The Adventures of Sinbad the Sailor

Retold by Katie Daynes

Illustrated by
Paddy Mounter

Reading Consultant: Alison Kelly
University of Surrey Roehampton

Contents

Chapter 1

Sinbad's first voyage

Long ago, in the city of
Baghdad, Sinbad lived with
his father, a rich merchant.
When the merchant died, he
left Sinbad his whole fortune.

3

Sinbad was so rich, he didn't need to work. Instead, he spent his money on fine clothes and wild parties.

Don't worry, everything's on me.

One day, he was shocked to find his purse empty.

"I can't believe I've spent my fortune!" he said to himself.

He decided to follow in his father's footsteps and sell things for a living. First, he sold his house. Then he bought some expensive silks and spices and went down to the port.

We're sailing to Basra, then out to sea.

A group of merchants were busy loading their ship. They invited Sinbad to join them and he jumped on board.

After a week at sea, they dropped anchor by a sandy island. They were cooking supper over a fire, when the ground began to tremble.

"We're on a whale!" cried the captain and swam to the ship. The others were flung into the sea as the whale flipped its tail and dived underwater.

Many men drowned, but Sinbad was lucky. He clung on to a wooden chest and floated through the night. At dawn, he landed on the shore of a distant island.

A man on horseback spotted Sinbad and took him to see his ruler, King Mahrajan.

Sinbad told the king about the whale. "Now I'm stranded far from home," he sighed.

"Work for me and I'll look after you," said the king.

One day, Sinbad was on duty at the port, when a captain came up to him.

"Sir, where can I sell these silks and spices?" he asked.

Sinbad was amazed. "I had some silk like that..." he said.

"Well, these silks belonged to a merchant called Sinbad," said the captain.

"I *am* Sinbad," cried Sinbad.

But I thought you'd drowned!

I drifted to safety.

The captain gave Sinbad his silks and spices. After selling them at an excellent price, Sinbad joined the captain's ship and set sail for Baghdad.

Chapter 2

Itchy feet

At first, Sinbad was delighted to be home. But soon he had itchy feet. He wanted to visit new places. So he bought more silks and spices to trade.

A friendly captain welcomed him on board his ship and they headed for the high seas.

This is the life!

One day, they stopped at a deserted island to collect fresh water. Sinbad sat down in a shady spot and fell asleep.

An hour later, he woke in a panic. The ship had set sail without him. He was stranded.

Sinbad climbed a tree and looked over the island. All he could see was one huge, white egg. As Sinbad watched, a gigantic bird flew onto the egg and settled down to sleep.

It must be a roc!

Sinbad knew the roc bird was very strong. Maybe it could rescue him. He unwound his turban, crept up to the bird and tied himself to its leg.

When the roc woke up, it
stretched its giant wings and
soared into the sky.

Sinbad found himself
dangling high above the clouds.

Gulp!

Before long, the roc dived
down into a deep valley.
Sinbad felt hard ground
beneath his feet and quickly
untied himself.

The roc caught a sheep in its claws and flew away. Sinbad stared in fear at the steep-sided valley. It was squirming with snakes, which slithered over dead sheep.

Then Sinbad noticed the ground was studded with jewels. He was stuffing some in his pockets, when he saw a vicious snake eyeing him hungrily.

Sinbad ducked down. How could he escape? Seeing the rocs circling overhead gave him an idea...

Quickly, he tied himself to a sheep and waited. In no time, a roc swooped down and grabbed the sheep in its claws. It flew out of the valley, with Sinbad trailing below.

The roc landed on a cliff. It was about to eat the sheep, when a group of men charged at the bird, scaring it away.

"Bother!" said one. "No jewels in *this* sheep's wool."

Then they spotted Sinbad. His escape from snake valley amazed them. In return for some jewels, they put him on a ship bound for Baghdad.

Chapter 3

The greedy giant

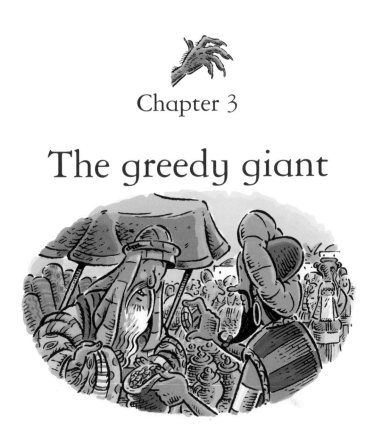

Once more, Sinbad was
delighted to be home. But the
feeling didn't last long. This
time, he traded a bag of jewels
for silks and spices to sell.

His third journey went well and land was in sight when a bunch of short, ugly and very hairy men ambushed the ship. One by one, the hairy men threw the merchants overboard, then sailed away.

How dare you take our ship!

The miserable merchants were washed onto a beach.

They explored the new shore
and found a courtyard filled
with pots and firewood.

But the courtyard was owned
by a greedy giant, who licked
his lips when he saw his visitors.
Before they could blink, he
roasted a fat merchant.

After supper, the giant fell asleep – across the only exit.

"Don't worry," whispered Sinbad. "When he leaves, we'll take his firewood and make a raft so we can escape."

At dawn, the giant woke up, heaved himself to his feet and left. The men hurried to the beach, where they tied the firewood together with vines.

As they pushed off from the shore, they heard a big splash. The angry giant was pelting the raft with rocks. Seconds later, a rock smashed the raft to pieces.

Aghh!

Most of the men drowned, but Sinbad and two others were lucky. They survived by clinging onto a log. But by noon, they had fainted under the hot sun.

The next thing they knew,
they had drifted onto a stony
beach and a huge snake had
wound itself around them. It
eyed the three men, opened its
mouth wide and swallowed
Sinbad's two friends.

Sinbad didn't dare move until
the snake had slithered off.

He gazed out to sea,
praying for a ship to arrive...
and one did! Better still,
Sinbad recognized the captain
from his second journey.

You left me stranded on a desert island!

Sorry about that.

Within a week, Sinbad was
back in Baghdad.

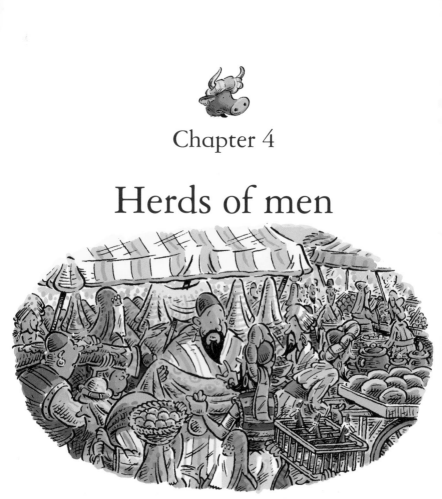

Chapter 4

Herds of men

"Home again!" cried Sinbad. But it didn't take long before he was back at the market, buying silks and spices.

He joined another merchant ship and traded his goods from port to port.

One day, a sudden gale whipped up the waves. Water came crashing onto the deck and smashed up the ship.

Sinbad and seven other merchants were luckier than the rest. They clung onto the broken mast and drifted to a far-off shore.

Some islanders found the men
and took them to their king.
"Welcome," said the king.
"Please join us for a feast."

Yum!

They were all starving,
except for Sinbad. He just
watched as the others gobbled
down food. To his horror, the
hungry men turned into
slurping, guzzling animals.

26

"Stop eating!" Sinbad cried, but the men no longer understood him. An islander rounded up Sinbad's friends and herded them through the door.

Sinbad hid in a dark corner. When no one was looking, he fled from the palace grounds.

He ran straight past the
herd of men, who were grazing
in a field. And he didn't stop
until he'd reached the other
side of the island.

I see a
sail!

There, he couldn't believe his
luck. A ship was sailing close
to shore. He waved at it wildly
and the captain waved back.
Soon, Sinbad was heading for
Baghdad again.

Chapter 5

The roc's revenge

The problem was Sinbad found life at home dull after his adventures. One morning he saw a beautiful new ship at the port and decided to buy it.

He loaded the ship with silks and spices, hired an eager crew and set sail.

They came to an island with another roc's egg. Some sailors were curious and went to see it. They threw stones at the egg to see how tough it was.

Fifty stones later, it cracked. "Fools!" cried Sinbad. "The mother roc will want revenge!"

As they sailed away, a dark shape hid the sun. It was a roc! She dropped a massive boulder on the ship and all but Sinbad perished in the sea.

31

Yet again, Sinbad was saved. This time, he was swept to a leafy island. As he paused for water by a stream, he saw a sad troll.

What's wrong?

Sinbad helped the troll cross the stream. But then the troll refused to get down from Sinbad's shoulders. It just tightened its grip around his neck.

For days, Sinbad was the troll's prisoner. He carried it everywhere until he was exhausted. Then he remembered he had a flask of wine.

The troll saw Sinbad take a sip and snatched the flask. It glugged down the wine and was soon swaying from side to side. A few burps later, it toppled to the ground.

33

Sinbad ran away
and met some people
carrying baskets. "Can you
help me get to Baghdad?" he
asked hurriedly.

"If you help us collect more
coconuts," replied a bald man.

"How?" wondered Sinbad,
following the group into a
forest of palms. Monkeys
chattered in every tree.

34

"Watch!" said the man. He picked up a stone and threw it at a monkey. The monkey was very annoyed and threw a coconut back at the man.

Hey! That nearly hit me.

Soon, all the monkeys were throwing coconuts. Sinbad easily collected enough to pay for his trip home.

35

Chapter 6

Risking the river

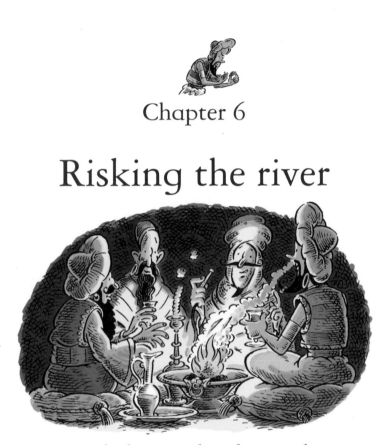

For a while, Sinbad was happy simply lazing around at home. Then some merchants came to visit and their tales of travel filled Sinbad with envy.

He set sail once more,
trading from port to port...

What a lovely, calm evening.

until one night, the ship sailed
off course. In the gloom, no
one saw sharp rocks ahead.
The ship was smashed to
pieces and only Sinbad and
four others reached the shore.

They searched the craggy island from top to bottom and found nothing but rocks and water. One by one, the men starved to death.

Before long, Sinbad was the only man left. He sat by a river, feeling very alone.

Then he noticed something strange. The river was flowing into a cave, not out to sea.

Sinbad had an idea. "I'll make a raft," he thought, "and hope the river leads me to some food."

The riverbed sparkled with jewels, so he took a few handfuls before floating off.

His raft glided into the cave and sped up, hurtling through darkness. All Sinbad could hear was the whoosh of water. Had his luck finally run out?

The next thing he knew, he was lying on a sunny bank. He looked up to see a crowd gathered around him.

A local merchant gave Sinbad some food and, in return for several jewels, sent him on a ship to Baghdad.

Chapter 7

The final voyage

Back home, Sinbad's jewels bought him all kinds of treats. But, guess what? Sinbad still wasn't content.

"Soon I'll be too old to travel," he thought.

So he set out on a final
journey. He was aboard a
merchant ship in the China
Sea when a terrible storm
blew up.

A monster whale surged up
through the waves. As it got
closer, it opened its massive
jaws and swallowed the ship
in one gulp.

Luckily, Sinbad managed to jump overboard just in time. The storm died down and, once again, he drifted to a strange shore.

Another close escape. I don't know how I do it!

As he wandered through an exotic forest, he found a river flowing into a cave.

"Aha! I'll build another raft," thought Sinbad.

43

But this river carried him through darkness to a steep waterfall.

"I'm a dead man!" Sinbad screamed, as he started falling.

That's a very big fish...

Suddenly, he stopped — in mid-air. A surprised old man had caught him in a net.

"You need to dry off!" said the man, and he took Sinbad home with him.

44

The old man asked his daughter, Emira, to fetch some clothes. Sinbad gazed at her open-mouthed. He had never seen such a lovely woman.

Thank you very much.

Emira's father thought Sinbad was charming and invited him to stay. Over the next few weeks, Emira and Sinbad fell in love.

With the old man's blessing, the couple married.

A year later, Emira's father died of old age, leaving her and Sinbad a fortune.

"Why don't we go sailing?" said Sinbad. "We could buy some silks and spices to trade."

"Ooh, yes!" replied Emira, who had always wanted to travel.

After months at sea, they found themselves in Baghdad.

"What a gorgeous city!" cried Emira.

"Isn't it!" agreed Sinbad. He was delighted to be home... at least for a while.

Sinbad comes from a collection of Arabian stories known as *The Thousand and One Nights*. According to legend, a Sultan wanted to kill his wife. To save herself, the wife started telling a wonderful story. The Sultan found the story so good, he let her live to finish it. Then she started another one. Hundreds of stories and 1001 nights later, the Sultan let his wife go.

Series editor: Lesley Sims
Designed by Russell Punter

First published in 2004 by Usborne Publishing Ltd., Usborne House, 83-85 Saffron Hill, London EC1N 8RT, England. www.usborne.com
Copyright © 2004 Usborne Publishing Ltd.